Another Sommer-Time Story

It's Not FAIR!

By Carl Sommer
Illustrated by Greg Budwine

Advance • HOUSTON
PUBLISHING INC

Permissions
Advance Publishing, Inc.
6950 Fulton St.
Houston, TX 77022

www.advancepublishing.com

First Edition
Printed in Singapore

Library of Congress Cataloging-in-Publication Data

Sommer, Carl, 1930-
   It's not fair! / by Carl Sommer ; illustrated by Greg Budwine.
      p. cm. -- (Another Sommer-Time Story)
   Summary: Buzzie becomes unhappy with her role as a worker bee and starts a revolt at her hive, until she discovers that working together is the best way to be happy.
      ISBN 1-57537-021-2 (hardcover: alk. paper) -- ISBN 1-57537-070-0 (library binding: alk. paper)
      [1. Bumblebees--Fiction. 2. Cooperativeness--Fiction.] I. Budwine, Greg, ill. II Title.
III. Series: Sommer, Carl, 1930- Another Sommer-Time Story.
PZ7.S696235 It 2003
[E]--dc21
                                                                          2002026167

It's Not FAIR!

In the forest there lived a colony of bees where everyone worked together as one happy family.

But one day, everything drastically changed. Buzzie, a young worker bee, stood at the door of her hive and said, "What a beautiful day! I wonder where I could go to gather pollen for our family?"

"I know," said Buzzie. "I'll go to the garden where I went yesterday."

Buzzie flew straight to the garden. But when she got there, she could not find any pollen. "Oh my!" she said. "The bees must have gathered all the pollen yesterday. But that's no problem. I'll just go elsewhere."

As Buzzie flew by a house, she saw some
flowers on a windowsill. "Oh good!" she said.
As she gathered pollen from the flowers, she

exclaimed, "This is great! These flowers have lots of pollen. I'll be able to take lots of food back to the hive."

Then Buzzie saw other flowers on the table. "Look at them!" she exclaimed.

Buzzie quickly flew to the other flowers. "This is great!" she said as she gathered the pollen. "These flowers also have lots of pollen. I can't wait to tell the other bees about my great find."

Danny and Mary came into the room. "It's chilly," said Mary. Danny walked over and closed the window.

When Buzzie heard the noise, she jumped. "What was that?" she asked. "I'd better get out of here fast." Buzzie dashed for the window.

BANG!!!! Buzzie hit the window full force and bounced back.

"OUCH!!!!" yelled Buzzie. She got up and tried again. She banged into the window and fell on the windowsill. Buzzie was *trapped*!

"How can I get out of here?" she wondered.

When Danny saw Buzzie, he said, "That's a foolish worker bee." Then he laughed and said, "Worker bees are girl bees. They do all the work."

Mary frowned and asked, "How do you know?"

"I read about them," said Danny. "This is what worker bees do:

    Remove stale air.

    Keep the hive at the right temperature.

    Gather all the food.

    Clean the cells in the hive.

Build the comb where honey is stored.
And guard the hive.

"But the queen bee just stays in the hive and lays eggs. She has worker bees feeding and taking care of her and her babies! And the boy drones just loaf around and wait until the queen needs them. Their job is the easiest."

Then Danny let out a loud roar of laughter. "Ha! Ha! Ha! Worker bees are surely foolish! They do ALL the work!"

Mary rolled her eyes at her brother and said, "I feel sorry for this poor worker bee. I'll open the window to let her fly out."

Mary opened the window and sighed, "Fly out, poor bee. You have lots of hard work to do."

When Buzzie saw the open window, she quickly flew out. "Whew!" she said. "That was scary!"

   Before this, Buzzie was a very happy bee. But Buzzie heard *everything* that Danny had said.

   As she flew back to the hive, she began complaining. "It's not *fair*! Why do we worker bees have to do all the work? We gather all the food, clean the cells, make the honeycomb, take care of the babies, feed the queen, air-condition the hive, and guard against enemies. All we do is work, work, work! It's not FAIR!"

The more Buzzie thought about it, the angrier she became. When she got back to the hive, she was *furious*.

When she met the worker bees guarding the hive, she exclaimed, "It's not *fair*! We worker bees have to do *all* the work."

"What do you mean?" asked a guard.

"Look at us," said Buzzie. "We..."

Just then a mouse stuck his head into the hive. "Attack!" yelled the guards.

Immediately, all the guards surrounded the mouse and yelled, "Get out of here!"

Then a guard named Tilly stuck the mouse with her stinger.

"Ouch!" screamed the mouse. He quickly spun around and left the hive. Then Tilly flew away and fell to the bottom of the hive and died.

One of the guards began to cry. "Poor Tilly. She had to die to protect the hive."

Then a guard asked Buzzie, "What were you saying?"

"Look at us poor workers!" complained Buzzie. "We gather all the food, clean the cells, make the honeycomb, take care of the babies, feed the queen, air-condition the hive, and guard against enemies. All we do is work, work, work! It's not FAIR!"

Then a guard named Fuzzy pointed to her stinger and explained, "When we use our stingers, like Tilly just did, we die. It's not *fair* that we have to give our lives for the hive."

"That's right!" complained all the young guards.

"Wait!" yelled Wizbee, the oldest bee. "It is fair! It's been proven—working with a leader brings happiness."

But Buzzie was not interested in what Wizbee had to say. She was furious.

She flew to the workers caring for the babies and those fanning the hive and complained. "Look at us poor workers. We gather all the food, clean the cells, make the honeycomb, take care

of the babies, feed the queen, air-condition the hive, and guard against enemies. All we do is work, work, work! It's not FAIR!"

"You're right," they said. Then all the young caretakers and fanners became angry and began complaining.

Then Buzzie announced, "Everyone who is unhappy, follow me! I know where we can start a new hive."

"Hoorayyyy!!!" yelled the young worker bees.

"Wait!" yelled Wizbee. "It *is* fair what we have! Let me explain it to you."

But the young bees were mad. They ignored Wizbee and flew out of the hive.

The angry bees followed Buzzie to a large oak tree. When they gathered together, Buzzie asked, "Does anyone have any ideas?"

They began offering suggestions. The smaller bees spoke first. "The bigger bees should guard the hive because they're the strongest."

"No!" yelled the bigger bees. "The smaller bees should be the guards. They fly the fastest."

And so it went. No one wanted to be a guard because they were afraid they might have to die. Everyone wanted what they thought was the easiest job—a fanner.

Then all the bees began arguing and yelling.
They got so loud that Buzzie finally screamed,
"Stop!!!! This is no way to have a happy hive."

"Who made you the leader over us?" a bee
screamed back.

"That's right!" yelled all the bees. "You're not
our leader!"

The bees continued to argue and yell. Then they began fighting with one another.

When Buzzie saw what was happening, she got so mad that she left. "What can I do?" she wondered. "Everyone refuses to work."

Then a thought flashed through her mind. "I'll ask one of the older bees what to do."

When Buzzie arrived at the hive, the older worker bees were happily working together. Buzzie flew to Wizbee and asked, "Do you have any suggestions on how we can have a happy hive? We're having lots of problems working together."

"Who is your leader?" asked Wizbee.

"We don't have a leader," mumbled Buzzie.

"You can't have a happy hive without a leader," explained Wizbee. "You need a queen bee."

"I never thought of that!" said a surprised Buzzie.

"Once you have a leader," explained Wizbee, "it's important to let the leader tell the other bees what kind of work they should do. This will stop all the complaining."

"You're right," said Buzzie. Then she threw her hands into the air and exclaimed, "That's what we had in our hive!"

"That's right," said Wizbee. "Everyone was happy until you started complaining."

"I'm sorry," said Buzzie, "Now I understand, working with a leader brings happiness. I'm flying back and telling the young workers that what we had was fair. Thank you for helping me."

Wizbee waved goodbye as Buzzie flew away.

As Buzzie flew back to the young workers, she said, "I'm so glad I asked Wizbee for advice. Now I know how we can have a happy hive." Then Buzzie began to sing this song:

Working together,
How happy we'll be.
Working and helping,
Big smiles we'll see.

When she came near the hive, she could hear
the bees arguing and complaining.

Buzzie flew into the midst of the noisy crowd and shouted, "Stop your arguing and fussing! I know how to have a happy hive."

Everyone stopped talking. "I'm sorry for complaining," said Buzzie. "If we want a happy hive, we need a leader like the queen bee. Then we

need to let the queen bee tell us what to do."

"That's right," said all the workers.

"To have future workers we need drone bees for the queen," explained Buzzie. "Then by working together, we'll have a happy hive."

"Buzzie," shouted a worker, "you're a genius!"

"I'm not a genius," said Buzzie. "We just need to obey our leader and work together."

"Let's go!" they all shouted. While flying back, they began singing this song:

Working together,
How happy we'll be.
Working and helping,
Big smiles we'll see.

When the bees arrived, they bowed their heads before the queen bee and said, "We're sorry for complaining."

"I forgive you," said the queen bee.

"Thank you," said the workers.

Then some young workers immediately went to gather pollen.

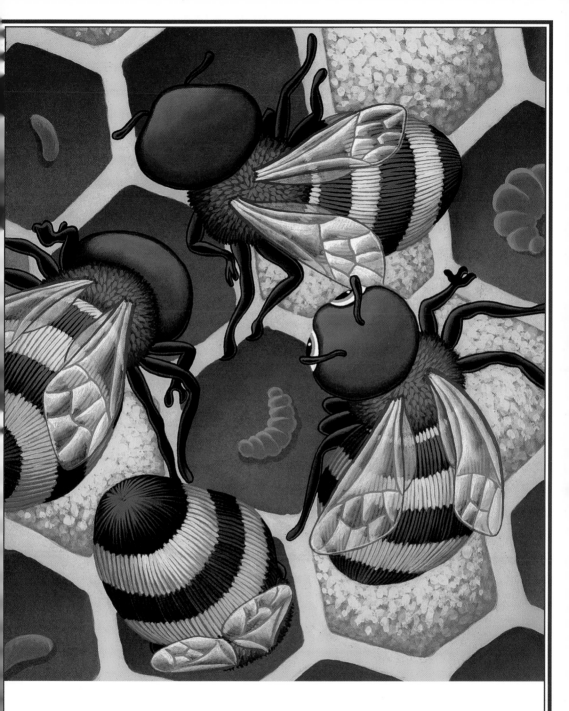

The caretakers said, "Let's do our job."
Immediately they began to clean the empty cells, feed the babies, and build the combs. They were so glad to be back in their hive again.

The guard bees said, "Let's go and protect the hive." They quickly flew to the entrance of the hive to guard against their enemies.

The fanners said, "Let's get the hive to the right temperature." Immediately they began flapping their wings.

That night Buzzie said to Wizbee, "You were right. Working together with a leader brings happiness."

From that day on, no bee ever complained about her work. And if any bee ever heard someone say, "Look at the poor worker bee," she would not listen. The bees knew that happy bees are those who obey their leader and work together.

Now whenever bees went looking for food, they
would sing this song:

> Working together,
> How happy we'll be.
> Working and helping,
> Big smiles we'll see.

Working Together

Words and Music
by Carl Sommer